SOS SAGAS

# TRAPPED

## Fearful Tales

Edited By Jenni Harrison

First published in Great Britain in 2021 by:

Young Writers
Remus House
Coltsfoot Drive
Peterborough
PE2 9BF
Telephone: 01733 890066
Website: www.youngwriters.co.uk

Printed and bound in the UK by BookPrintingUK
Website: www.bookprintinguk.com
YB0458F

# FOREWORD

**IF YOU FIND YOU'RE GETTING BORED OF READING THE SAME OLD THING ALL THE TIME, YOU'VE COME TO THE RIGHT BOOK. THIS ANTHOLOGY IS HERE TO BREAK YOU OUT OF YOUR READING RUT AND GIVE YOU GRIPPING ADVENTURES, TALES OF SUSPENSE AND IMAGINATIVE WRITING GALORE!**

We challenged secondary school students to craft a story in just 100 words. In this third installment of our SOS Sagas, their mission was to write on the theme of 'Trapped'. They were encouraged to think beyond their first instincts and explore deeper into the theme. The result is a variety of styles and genres and, as well as some classic tales of physical entrapment, inside these pages you may find characters trapped in relationships, struggling with mental health issues, or even characters who are the ones doing the trapping.

Here at Young Writers it's our aim to inspire the next generation and instill in them a love of creative writing, and what better way than to see their work in print? The imagination and skill within these pages are proof that we might just be achieving that aim! Well done to each of these fantastic authors.

# CONTENTS

Theo McKeown (12) 65
Maria Baum (11) 66

## Rosebery School, Epsom

Zoe de Palma (12) 67
Sylvie Martin (12) 68
Emma Glencross (13) 69
Lauren Light (12) 70

## Ysgol Garth Olwg, Church Village

Branwen Parker (11) 71
Tia Edwards (11) 72
Thea-Grace Sims (12) 73
Megan Evans (11) 74
Catrin Fowler (11) 75
Alice Hanks-Doyle (12) 76
Sasha Gardiner (12) 77
Begw Williams (11) 78
Cadi Evans (12) 79
Violet Hammerton (13) 80
Amy Hammond (12) 81
Hanna Rees (12) 82
Gwennan Deavall (12) 83
Brynley Davies (11) 84
Isla Powell (12) 85
Brooke Ward (11) 86
Tamia Davis (11) 87
Owen Jenkins (11) 88
Lauren Knight (12) 89
Talis Vining (12) 90
Jessica Mills (12) 91
Keilan Bryn Harris (12) 92
Caitlin Rees (11) 93
Alys Williams (12) 94
Harry Barrett 95
Tomas Norcup (12) 96
Finlay Hawkins (11) 97
Ellie Ryan (12) 98
Sophia Grace Goulding (12) 99
Grace Hawkins (12) 100
Charlotte Royle (15) 101
Tomos Pritchard (11) 102

George Baldwin (12) 103
Oliver Andrzej Jenkins (11) 104
Gruff McCallionn (11) 105
Sam May (11) 106
Daniel Wright (11) 107
Anika Richards (11) 108
Lola Pugh (11) 109
Freddy Gabe-Williams (11) 110
Dylan Corsi (12) 111
Ifan Harris (12) 112
Seren Kyte (12) 113
Evan McCarthy (12) 114
Morgan Pugh (11) 115
Harri Tudor-Asveld (11) 116
Madison Ranson (12) 117
Chloe Edmunds (11) 118
Noah Daniell (11) 119
Awen Rhys (11) 120
Scarlett Chard (11) 121
Ffion Jenkins (11) 122
Rhys White (11) 123
Isabella Fry (11) 124
Lewis Pitman (12) 125
Freya Scofield (12) 126
Evie Rock (12) 127
Harrison Keetch (12) 128
Ehran Richards (11) 129
Lilly Davies (11) 130
Max McDonagh (11) 131
Mali Cotter (12) 132
Gethin Brooke (11) 133
Sophia Smith (11) 134
Will Thomas (11) 135
Daniel Jones (12) 136
Megan Phillips (11) 137
Lexie Wright (11) 138
Thomas English (12) 139
Eleri Gardner (12) 140
Dylan Griffiths (12) 141
Seren Smith (12) 142
Jac Lewis (12) 143
Harrison Thomas (13) 144
Alex Rutherford (12) 145

| | |
|---|---|
| Gwenllian Hadley (11) | 146 |
| Lydia Higgins (12) | 147 |
| Elliott Barrett (11) | 148 |
| Ruben Lewis (12) | 149 |
| Menna Owen (11) | 150 |
| Elliw Porter (11) | 151 |
| Lillie Thomas (11) | 152 |
| Dan Thomson (11) | 153 |
| Ablah McBean (11) | 154 |
| Alfie O'Keefe (11) | 155 |
| Alexa-Rae Jones (11) | 156 |
| Harri Jones (12) | 157 |
| Maisie Westall (12) | 158 |
| Eva Mason (11) | 159 |
| Evan Smith (11) | 160 |
| Samson Dossett (11) | 161 |
| Joshua Capper (12) | 162 |
| Eva Thomas (11) | 163 |
| Nathan Evans (11) | 164 |
| Connor Gee-Wing (11) | 165 |
| Gwenllian Campion (12) | 166 |
| Sam Price | 167 |
| Alice Bell (11) | 168 |
| Grace Huish (11) | 169 |
| Lani Jones (11) | 170 |
| Gracie Nuthall (11) | 171 |
| Siôn Bowen (11) | 172 |
| Nia Akers (11) | 173 |
| Keelan Hatton (11) | 174 |
| Sophie Poucher (11) | 175 |
| Callum Hooper (11) | 176 |
| Louisa Royle (11) | 177 |
| Jack Pidd (11) | 178 |
| Leila Jones (12) | 179 |
| Olivia Bell (11) | 180 |
| Brooklin Baldwin (11) | 181 |
| Gareth Church (12) | 182 |
| Finnley Walker (11) | 183 |
| Hannah Weston (11) | 184 |
| Dylan Szalkowski (11) | 185 |
| Mari Roberts (11) | 186 |
| Anwen Winter (11) | 187 |
| Lily Reid (12) | 188 |

# THE STORIES

# Trapped All Alone, Nowhere To Go

Trapped, all alone nowhere to go. Overpowering bangs and booms were all you could hear. Trapped, day in, day out. Freedom, I'd give anything to leave this tormenting, traumatising place I found myself in.

Smoke filled the air, people wearing gas masks were trying to leave this horrible foggy environment. I walked around looking for Mum and realised I'd travelled to a different world. I came to the realisation I was not dreaming, it was real. I wasn't in 2020, I was in 1917.

I hesitated, what was special about the year 1917? Could it be I was in WWI?

**Abigail Luffman (11)**
Bushey Meads School, Bushey

# Trapped

The box was filling with water. I started panicking, my fists merely bruising the glass prison. The water was engulfing my knees. Time was running out. I started imagining the worst, would I die? No, sto- Giggling. It was getting louder, like a bomb ticking in my brain. I thought they cared, guess I was wrong. It was travelling up my neck, like a lion stalking its prey. "Let me out!" I screamed as my mouth and nose were taken. I started striking harder... Then, it shattered. I was flushed out... darkness. I woke. The box was filling with water.

## Luca Irimia (12)
Bushey Meads School, Bushey

# The Beast

We're watching, we always are... Movement! I crept over, weapon at the ready. Suddenly, low growls filled the air. I turned around. My ally had taken care of the threat, or so I thought. I kept moving. *Snap!* went a twig. I smiled, then followed the sound. I smelt something bad, it came from my shoe! Poo. It was fresh. I stood up and looked. A beast covered in fur, sharp teeth, sharp claws. It jumped me. Its master came from the shadows. "Thought you could escape did you?" said the police officer. I was sent back to my cell.

## Isaac Mallon (12)
Bushey Meads School, Bushey

# Back To The Future

T-minus 5... 4... 3... 2... 1! Instantly I'm teleported to the past. I awake to the noise of loud bangs and firing guns. I run out of the rubble and towards an air raid shelter. *Boom!* goes another bomb! I'm geared up, handed a gun and forced to fight. More shots fired! Confusion, fear, panic, a whirlwind of emotions in my head. Men shouting, sirens wailing. Smoky Spitfires zoom by and I realise I'm a soldier in WWII! My world shattering, my mind spinning. Where do I- *Bang!* Am I hit? I am hit! Help! I'm trapped!

## Yasir Khan (12)
Bushey Meads School, Bushey

# Trapped

The clock ticked and tocked as I waited in anticipation for what was going to happen next. I clenched my fists to resist the urge to grasp the handle that was barely out of reach. An overwhelming impulse to run took over my concentration. I started to spiral and lose my train of thought. *Bang!* An acorn collided against the tin roof causing everyone to panic. As the chatter rose so did my anxiety. Suddenly a bell rang and everyone stood to their feet, cheering. As if my life depended on it, I raced out of class to sweet freedom.

## Polly Pryra (12)
Bushey Meads School, Bushey

# Dead

Swim, that's all I do, swim. Their huge eyes peered at me, piercing my soul. Finally they opened the food. I hadn't been fed in days. The mushy substance dropped down and I took a bite of hell. It's been another few days without food. Argh! A weird sensation entered my body. I dropped to the bottom of the tank, the stones flying up around me. Suddenly the tank tipped. I heard them all scream and cry. I looked up and there were my tormentors. I wished for death. Finally, relief and the pain stopped. Then the world went black.

**Sophie Cohen (12)**
Bushey Meads School, Bushey

# Trapped

I clambered into the forest, the dank air pushing me back as I ventured forward. They were everywhere: ahead, behind, to the side. Humanoid figures festooned the trees. They stared at me. Canisters lay in their arms. They let out what they held. Black.

I woke in a ship of some sort with straps on my limbs. A man walked in with an injection and stabbed it through my skin. I saw the truth. Humanity polluted the universe. They had to be converted into the true human. We would hunt them down. One by one. Their end is coming soon.

**Joseph Gill (11)**
Bushey Meads School, Bushey

# Trapped

The lift suddenly stopped, my gut dropped. I looked around to see what was happening. I was all alone. No one to help me. The lift stayed still. I felt sweat, the walls were closing in, the lights flickered, and suddenly darkness. I couldn't see a thing. I cried for help. I was stuck on the top floor of a building, all alone, in a pitch-black lift. And then something broke. The lift started dropping. It was falling so fast, I could barely think about what was happening. This was it, this was the end. I had been trapped.

**Lila Krikler (12)**
Bushey Meads School, Bushey

# Trapped

They were watching, they always were. It was a game between life and death. We all stood there terrified. My heart was pounding. I took in the moment, thinking it was the last time I would hear it. I clenched my dagger, ready to live with the guilt, that is if I lived. My stomach clenched. My teeth were chattering on this cold winter's morning. I was wishing this was just a nightmare, a really bad nightmare, but I knew better. This was real. I was not ready to die. I wasn't. The bell rang and the game had started.

**Roma Savjani (12)**
Bushey Meads School, Bushey

# Me And You

So, it's just you and me here. You must be my brain. It's a pleasure to meet you. It's kinda quiet in here, when I'm not listening that is. I like it. Just me and you. I heard them you know. I won't wake up. I don't mind. Just me and you. You nad me forever. No more suffering and toxic friends and addiction. No more except you, true love. This is life where I'm meant to be. They will give up soon. The beeping will stop. Then we can be alone forever. No escape. You're trapped. Just like me.

## Lana Wurr (12)
Bushey Meads School, Bushey

# Caged

People stare, people point as I cower away in the corner, admiring my every move. I hate it. All I've ever wished for is freedom, day in, day out. Every day the keepers come to let my wings spread for a bit. I try to escape, but I never succeed. The visitors' eyes burn through my skin, making me feel self-conscious every minute of every hour. Suddenly, I realise the lock on the door has come loose. I spread my wings and fly. I think to myself, was the lock actually loose, was it magic or did someone open it?

**Louisa Winslett (11)**
Bushey Meads School, Bushey

# Trapped In A Cage...

It's been 1,246 days. I'm being stared at every minute, every second. I can't leave at all, even if I need the toilet. The only reason I could go outside was when I needed to go for my daily exercise or to go and eat my meals. This is torture. The people that were watching me were really rude guards. I'm trying to figure out what I have done. All I remembered was that someone dragged me by the arms. They put me into some kind of dirty old cage. Maybe some day I could escape and leave this place.

**Julia Bielinska (12)**
Bushey Meads School, Bushey

# Trapped On A Train

Suddenly I woke up and it was dark as the night sky. I could hear a strange noise but couldn't make it out, I almost felt like I was trapped. It was like an endless tunnel that you could never get out of. Eventually I noticed that I was on a train. I kept walking until I found a flashlight. Sooner or later I knew I was going to go crazy, but I kept going. Suddenly the flashlight stopped working and the strange noises stopped. I couldn't see a thing except pitch-black darkness. After that, it went blank.

**Alfie Smith (12)**
Bushey Meads School, Bushey

# Trapped In An Aquarium

I've been taken from my home and imprisoned. I'm trapped. I'm here in this prison with some of my friends. People come to visit me every day, they tap on the glass when I least expect it. I get fed twice a day and someone comes in and cleans the glass. He scares me a lot but I don't tell my friends that. I really miss my mum and dad. I miss being with them and eating with them. I remember being taken, I was playing with my friends in the ocean and a net came over. That was torture.

## Leo Fearnside (11)
Bushey Meads School, Bushey

# Trapped In A Cage

I felt lonely, scared, depressed, unloved, trapped. All because I was locked in this tiny cage with no way of escaping. So what happened was I was with all my friends in this huge cage then me and one of my friends were taken somewhere, and that place was a new home. It was barricaded in these weird metal bars, hardly any water but plenty of food to last us a lifetime. We had the smallest running wheel, every time I used it my back ached. We had some hay. I just really needed a miracle to happen.

**C.J. May-Petrie (11)**
Bushey Meads School, Bushey

# Trapped

I'm trapped in this big car. I can't do anything while being trapped in a crisp packet. As well as not moving I can't call a human to come open the car door and take me out of the car and put me back where I belong. I wanted to be picked because I thought it was going to be fun but instead I've been left in the car with my buddies. I had many chances to escape from this rusty car but I couldn't move. Wait, do you hear that? Oh wait, it is just the crisp packet.

## Enoch Ansa-Otu (11)
Bushey Meads School, Bushey

# Trapped

I was a Hermann tortoise wandering around. Later on, I got caught by a gargantuan, mean, feisty hunter. I tried to escape as fast as I could but I was too slow. The hunter caught me and then caged me. I went screaming for help. I called my owner TJ, but he was too far. I screamed as loud as I could but he couldn't hear me. Then I whistled as loud as I could, and he finally heard me. I asked him to call the RSPCA. After they came I was set free. Now I am back with TJ.

## Maanav Shah (11)
Bushey Meads School, Bushey

# How My Life Was Changed

I saw the opponent coming up, we ran towards them but I saw a fist come towards my face. *Bang!* I woke up in some sort of metal box that was moving, bumping up and down. Eventually it stopped. Someone opened the door, it was a young man in uniform. That's when I realised I was captured by my opponent. He took me inside and up some stairs to some cells. He locked me up. Now this is where I've been ever since. I will never forget that day.

**Leon O'Reilly (11)**
Bushey Meads School, Bushey

# Captive

I watched her struggle. A sinister smirk grew on my face. "You can leave y'know." The victim rolled her eyes. I strolled around the fidgeting figure. "Such a... calming sight." Tears started streaming down her distressed face. I slowly crouched down to her level. "Why're you crying?" I pouted jokingly. "It's not gonna help." I stood up. "Now how would you like to pass. Fire, strangulation?" I sniggered. "Sorry, forgot you couldn't talk." I turned serious. "Stand." She stood. I harshly nudged her to the edge of the building's roof. "Say goodbye." I pushed her. "And don't tell anyone! Thanks!"

## Grace Castledine (11)
Caludon Castle School, Wyken

# Trapped

We waited and waited until a scream crept its way through the hallway, cursing our ears. "Well then look who finally woke up."
"Please, I-I don't know what you want. Please!"
"Huh, I'm not going to kill you you're going to do that yourself! Ha ha ha!"
"I need something, some...one."
Time passed. Nothing. The 'shadows of death' let non escape and I was about to find that out the hard way.
"Welcome to the shadows." The fallen light didn't really speak, Death did that for them. I was able to slip out the chains and hide.
"Rise."
"Argh!"

## Drew Mistry (11)
Caludon Castle School, Wyken

# Welcome To Jurassic World

"Welcome to Jurassic World!" That's what they said to us at the start of camp. We were trapped on this island full of dinosaurs. A clicking came from the forest.
"Velociraptor," a boy said. "A deadly hunter." Footsteps came from the forest. A giant female raptor with scars and on her teeth was blood. Human blood. She jumped on the flipped car. She pounced on the oldest boy. The boy screamed. The others ran to a small building. The screaming stopped. "The raptor's coming to eat us!" the boy screamed. The raptor roared and jumped through the window. Goodbye everyone.

**Luke Mcilhone (13)**
Caludon Castle School, Wyken

# Trapped And Kidnapped

I woke up and saw the most terrifying thing ever! "Argh!" I screamed. "Who are you?"

"You don't need to know who I am, you need to know that you're kidnapped and you're staying here until you die, which is only a couple of days."

"I'm Jonathan Smith, I don't know who you think I am."

"So you're not Bill Smith?"

"No!"

"I've got to tell the boss." And off he went. I only had a couple of minutes to think of a plan. That's when I thought of it. I cut through and I was out.

## Viraj Lad (12)
Caludon Castle School, Wyken

# When, Where, How?

I hear their faint words calling me... luring me... "Jack, Jack!" But I cannot answer, I'm stuck. Not sure where, not sure when, not sure how. The black abyss is closing in on me and somehow it's comforting. I have to remember what happened to me. "Jack." I was walking down the street. "Jack." I was on my way to tennis. "Jack." I was only a little away, maybe two or three steps away. "Jack!" My name was louder now. "Jack!" Very loud. Wait, I need to stay alive. "Jack!" A car, that's it.
I'm in a coma!

**Ella-May Hobley-Flitcroft (12)**
Caludon Castle School, Wyken

# The Call

*Bring, bring.* "You are the first, the start of the chain," he said, petrifying me. "You have two options. One, kill a stranger that you don't know, or two, we will kidnap you and kill you." He hangs up.
*Bring, bring.* "Have you made your choice?"
Petrified, I quivered then I chose. I still hate my choice. "I... I... want to choose one."
*Bring, bring, bring bring,* as I struggled to open my phone to answer I heard a car speeding past me. The car swerved and two men dragged me in and knocked me out cold.

## Dylan Beasley (12)
Caludon Castle School, Wyken

# Trapped!

She was trapped, stuck, the darkness surrounding her. She couldn't escape no matter where she went. She was trapped. The noises filled up her head. *Crack, bang, crash.* The noises were everywhere. The sound of her feet slammed against the floor as she ran, echoing around the cave. "Right, left, left," she whispered under her breath, but still she could not escape the noises still following her wherever she went. She was trapped. A shadow that was not hers started to run across the cave. *Grrr* she heard as it bounced from wall to wall like a tennis ball.

**Sally Watson (12)**
Caludon Castle School, Wyken

# The Cave

Lost. Forgotten. Abandoned. After centuries of being solo I had been discovered and my secrets revealed. I was never going to be alone again. They trekked through my towering corridors, into my desolate chambers and round my bottomless crater-like pits. How did they find me? Why were they here? What did they want? Glancing back at the tunnel they had come through they cautiously lumbered on, unaware of any dangers or what lay ahead. A deafening scream pierced my insides; one of the men had fallen down my opening. Painfully, he felt around only to realise... he was trapped.

## Rhiannon Rout (11)
Caludon Castle School, Wyken

# Trapped

Trapped 1,142 days, months, years I've been trapped in this very basement with the others. All of us, all thirty, have been trapped, taken from our families. By him. His name's Jimmy. He's kept us down here for years. I'm lucky I somehow haven't starved after only consuming crumbs and a tiny sip of water each day. But today that will change. Me and the other children have made a plan. We could try to etch, then smash a hole in the window as we haven't cut our nails forever. 3, 2, 1, *crash!* The window. We're saved. We're free.

**Finn West (13)**
Caludon Castle School, Wyken

# Trapped

I can not see! I can not hear! I can only feel the stone-cold floor beneath my numb, bare feet. I am alone, I am always alone. A shiver crawls down my spine and my eyes dart frantically around the spacious room looking for something, anything. Pounding my head is a time bomb waiting to explode. My thoughts dance around my brain like a deranged ballerina waiting in the wings. Powerfully, a rush of adrenaline shoots through my tortured body like a bullet fired from a shocked soldier's gun. I blink, gazing into the emptiness around me. I'm trapped!

**Amelie Bridges (12)**
Caludon Castle School, Wyken

# Trapped

Every day I do nothing. There's nothing I can do, nothing I want. I can't get up. I can't make myself get up. I can't make myself do anything. I'm trapped in darkness. Can't this just end? I can't move. I can't stand this. There's so much I could do, but I choose to do nothing. This is my choice, isn't it? I can't speak, I can't even scream. I can't move, I can't speak, I can't scream. I can't see. This isn't my choice. It can't be. Or is it? How did I get here? I need to think...

**Emma Griffiths (12)**
Caludon Castle School, Wyken

# The Shallows

I was in a cage. Trapped. I enjoyed the quietness, the noise of the water and the fish swimming around. I enjoyed being trapped. It was an escape from the outside world. I was shark caging down at the bay but it didn't feel right. Suddenly, I heard a click. The padlock seemed to have... opened. A great white shark came slowly slithering up to me. I tried to scream, but everything went black. "Avery? Avery! Wake up!" said a faint shrieking voice. My vision slowly got clearer. It was my sister followed by a lifeguard. My eyes shut again...

**Leah Woodhead (12)**
Caludon Castle School, Wyken

# Prepare For Impact

"Attention! This is your Captain speaking. Fasten your seatbelts and prepare for impact." My heart sank. I fumbled at my seatbelt trying to fasten it but then I felt a sharp sickness in my stomach. Screams of other passengers blocked out the sound of the wind going by. It was then I realised, my plane was crashing down into the ocean. Further and further we went down. Looking out the window, I saw one of the plane's engines completely on fire! My heart was pounding out of my chest. My hands shaking rapidly. I knew that it was all over...

**Lauren Wall (13)**
Caludon Castle School, Wyken

# Kill To Be Killed

As players panicked in fear of death, I looked around for a way to escape. The game creator announced, "If you die you will stay in this world forever! To get out of Kill or be Killed you'll have to kill the other players and be the last one standing. It's either kill or be killed. Let the battle... begin!" It was now or never. I could be stuck in the virtual world forever. "Argh!" What was that? I turned around frantically and saw my worst nightmare. Behind me was a girl with a crimson blade injected into her heart.

**George Abraham (12)**
Caludon Castle School, Wyken

# Alone

I woke up. That's what I saw. Nothing... nowhere... no one. I sat there wondering what happened before I blacked out. I couldn't remember. So, I sat there trying to remember. Still nothing. To make sure no one was here I shouted hello. Nothing. I sat there thinking... I was alone. Not only in here but when I'm at home or places like that. I thought about this and asked *why? Why am I alone?* Then I thought... *why do people hate me? Why? I have done nothing wrong to these people.* So now I sit here crying. Sigh. Why?

## Igor Kulka (11)
Caludon Castle School, Wyken

# In My Own Mind

Is it just me or is everyone looking at me? No, they can't be. Can they? It's fine, no one's watching me. Or are they? What if they are planning to follow me and find out where I live then kidnap me? It's okay, breathe. Someone is walking past, what do I do? Do I smile? Do I say nothing? Ahh why can't I stop thinking all this stuff? I feel like I'm suffocating. No, I'm trapped. Trapped in my own mind. My own thoughts. And I can't get out. They're getting closer. Should I turn? What are they planning?

**Lauren Buswell (12)**
Caludon Castle School, Wyken

# The Dreaming Football

Yesterday I was a human, today I am a football. As I sit and wait in the middle of the pitch, shocked and ready to be kicked I ask myself *is this a trick?* I couldn't move, I couldn't see, only imagine what must have happened. *Kick!* The whistle blew, the game had started. I went flying to another player's foot. As I flew immediately again a gasp from the crowd appeared, then went so silent I wondered if they'd disappeared. Then a roar could be heard. It was 1-0 to the team. How would I survive this?

**Rhylan James (13)**
Caludon Castle School, Wyken

# The Call Of The Torturer

I'd made sure to lock the doors tighter this time. With blood dripping off my hands, I wondered if what I was doing was right - of course it was, they deserved it for what the torture they'd put me and so many other children through. Miss Lavender (my neighbour) looked terrified as I came out of my house. I quickly checked my coat and realised the tiny speck of blood. In that moment I remembered the screams of my victims... and laughed. Then I knew what I had to do. I edged closer and closer as she screamed, horrified.

**Lily Hart (11)**
Caludon Castle School, Wyken

TRAPPED - FEARFUL TALES

# The Screams From Within

It was petrifying. An eleven-year-old girl trapped in an asylum during a zombie apocalypse. No biggie. It wasn't until I heard the blood-curdling screams that I started to panic. The fumes, oh boy the fumes. It smelled like rotten eggs in here. A sword of wind infected my skin. I heard glass breaking. The zombies were breaking in. I had no idea what to do. 1,142 days I've been in here. You'd think I'd be used to it by now. I found the broken window. I couldn't see any zombies. I was never going back there!

**Eleni Maoudis (11)**
Caludon Castle School, Wyken

# Sleeping Consciously

My eyes slowly adjust to the dark gloom of my room. No early morning rays of light slip through my blinds. Sleepy eyes drift around the room, until they land on my TV. The noise of static fills my ears. My first instinct is to switch it off yet for some reason I can't move. My body is slowly being consumed by panic. It's as if I'm not awake, nor asleep. My mind must be tricking me because I see a slim figure crouching by the TV. Lightning and thunder getting louder, wind gushing heavier and colder. All until...

## Imogen Seaton (12)
Caludon Castle School, Wyken

# Ghost In The House

Blue pushed me through the hole in the roof. I fell onto the bone and I felt it pierce through my back, but that's all I felt including the pain, because then everything went black. Now all I could do was wander around, hoping for my revenge against the rude little raptor who caused my death. One of the things that hurt the most was the fact that I was trapped in a house, watching the other dinosaurs getting all their freedom. So I scouted the place and I found someone. My friend, my secret deceptively kept brother...

## Alisheba Raza Jafri (12)
Caludon Castle School, Wyken

# My Nightmare

I couldn't move. I was stuck. I could hear screams of people dying into ashes. I was attached to my nightmare. Why, why, why? Why do I have to be the only one having this torture in the gloomy night? Suddenly I was trapped in eerie darkness. Would I survive or not? The only thing I could hear was the sound of my own breath mixing with the air. Wait! Footsteps were creeping around the room. I felt hesitant and terrified. I was going to die! *Boom!* I opened my eyes and saw my desk. Yay! Wait, what? Oh no!

## Saniya Ranjan (11)
Caludon Castle School, Wyken

# The Child Who Was Trapped

1,147 days I've been trapped here, in this very basement and this is the day I escape. The one who shall not be named comes down every night to give me food and sometimes a little conversation. But today at 12am I will do it. Only thirty seconds until... *Boom!* goes the window as I shot through it with the gun I found in a box. I'm to move quick as I can already hear footsteps coming from upstairs. I sprint up the boxes I put there earlier and finally I'm free. Home, that is where I am going to.

**Ella Tognonato (12)**
Caludon Castle School, Wyken

# The Dog Meat Trade

Trapped. Lost in the dark abyss of time. Maybe gone forever. I don't know where I am or who these other animals are, but this is not good. I haven't been fed for days, I'm dehydrated and homesick! Who sent me here? Also this is not a comfortable position. All I remember is a man with a mask broke in and gave me an injection near my collar. I don't think he was a vet? Then I blacked out... Now I'm here. I don't know for how long but I'm trapped in the abyss of time. Maybe for eternity...

**Charly Dade (12)**
Caludon Castle School, Wyken

# As I Sit Here...

Dear Diary, as I sit here, on the duck boards, writing this my mind is swirling with realist thoughts. Am I going to survive? As I sit here, I wonder if my friends are okay up there, fighting. As I sit here, listening to the bangs, crashes and screams my hope starts to diminish. Will I see my family again? I remember the last time I went above. All I saw was agony and fear. Above the trenches I was in constant fear of taking my last step. As the agonising flashbacks continue. I feel trapped in this terrifying war.

## Jenna May Bicknell (13)
Caludon Castle School, Wyken

# The Magic Box

It was going so well. It was our 100th time doing the trick. We practised every day and didn't take a break until it was all perfect. It was a busy morning. I got up at 6:30am, had breakfast and got dressed into my first costume. I collected everything we needed and waited for Chloe. She arrived in her little Mini and we drove to our destination. When we arrived I set up our tricks. We began. We flew through the first few tricks and before we knew it, we were on our famous box trick. I was trapped! Help!

**Hollie Weaver (13)**
Caludon Castle School, Wyken

# The Circus

I was stuck with clowns walking around me like I was a test subject. There were weird noises as the storm was getting closer. My heart was racing like a drum. I had a phobia of clowns! The clown started coming right into my face and I tried to run away but every door was superglued shut. Then a giant elephant came out and was inching closer to me on a red ball, so I sprinted up to the seats. But there were loads of clowns hiding behind the seats. My heart was pounding like a drum beating considerably.

**Renèe Clayton (11)**
Caludon Castle School, Wyken

# Sea Struck

Crystal-clear waves crashed to the ocean front. It was just the day to sail. I set sail as the gorgeous dun rose. As I sailed into blue heaven I saw a cave parallel to my direction. Soon the cave was in front of me. As I entered reluctantly, bubbles surrounded my boat. Trapped in the cave I started to paddle back to the start. In the blink of an eye I was panting for a single breath. My hands shook as I lifted the boat over without thinking. I followed the light. As I followed the light, I was out!

**Simran Bhatoa (13)**
Caludon Castle School, Wyken

# Locked In

1,142 days I've been here. Trapped in this body. Everything continues around me and I just long to go out and explore. I lay here listening, watching everyone around me. I try as hard as I can to move, to do everyday things, to speak but the more I try the more I fail. I feel like a baby, constantly being mothered, fed and teased. If I'm honest, I would rather be set to rest than stuck in this stupid body, not being able to interact with my loved ones. I just want to go home. I am trapped.

**Summer Roper (13)**
Caludon Castle School, Wyken

# School Of Spirits

As the bell rang for the end of the day, the doors shut as the spirits awoke. Ghosts were flying as the zombies lifted from the ground. As footsteps spread across the room, one thing caught my eye. The headteacher was flying. My heart beat as fast as ever. I had never been so scared. Then the steps came to an end. I turned around slowly. As I turned my life flashed before my eyes. I knew my life would end soon. And there it stood, it was me. I was alone and dying. I was alone, dying and trapped.

**Darcey White (11)**
Caludon Castle School, Wyken

# Trapped

The lift stopped suddenly. Was it planned? Did someone plot against me? The emergency button was broken and I couldn't call for help. What was I going to do? I was isolated from the rest of the world. My phone's battery was dead. What should I do? I was trapped. I tried to push the lift's door but it was colossal. Suddenly I heard footsteps behind me. The sound was coming closer and closer. I could finally see the guy's face. He was... he was... I could not believe my eyes...

**Abdel Alam (11)**
Caludon Castle School, Wyken

# Now You're Mine

I tiptoed round, not a sound. Then I saw it, the monster. It let out a loud shriek whilst I grabbed it and ran. Back at my house it started to cry for help. Then the angel on my left shoulder said, "Let it go," but the devil on my right said, "Keep it..." And with me the devil's always right. I went to go and get bread and water to keep it alive. When I came back it was gone! The next thing I knew... "FBI! Open up!" Where do I go, do I run or hide?

**Millie Melia (11)**
Caludon Castle School, Wyken

# The Screaming Girl

As I walked down the corridor, sweat was dripping down my forehead. I heard a little girl screaming. I was very keen to see what it was. I came to a door, it was getting louder and louder. I was hesitant to open it but curiosity got the better of me so I went to put my hand on the handle but suddenly, the door creaked open and I looked around in terror as lights flicked to black. I turned around and saw a terrified-looking girl staring right back at me. She started to walk towards me...

**Ava Moore (11)**
Caludon Castle School, Wyken

# Trapped

I'm trapped in a very, very big room that has only one window, and that one window is at the other end of the room. Getting to the window is hard. There are a lot of traps on the way. The first trap you have to try not to get impaled on a very long stick and then the next one you have to get past millions of bear traps without getting touched by one. If you get touched by one then millions of wasps the size of bananas will come and sting you to death, and then that's it.

**Jacob Kennell (12)**
Caludon Castle School, Wyken

# Trapped

It was one minute left till death, but I'd been planning for this for over a year. I've been breaking the bars of my cell. This was the day I'd escape. I could hear the guards coming, I needed to go now. I pushed the window bars out and crawled through the gap and ran away. I paid off a tower guard to not sound the alarm on the day of the escape. I climbed up the tower and down the rope. The alarm sounded but I was gone by then. I hopped in a car and off I went.

**Liam Mulvenna (11)**
Caludon Castle School, Wyken

# The Mysterious Disappearance

I was in my car following a family of four in their Citreon Picasso. I only noticed them because I was passing them on the motorway. Inside I saw an eleven-year-old and a five-year-old, I think they were at least. There was a girl and another girl. Oh, I'm Jimmy by the way, Jimmy Savle.
I got to the hotel where they were staying, the parents were out. I climbed in and nabbed the first one I saw, it was the younger one. I took her to my van. She was trapped.

**Kai Kenion (13)**
Caludon Castle School, Wyken

# Kidnapped

Trapped in the back of a van, tape over my mouth, hands tied up. Kidnapped. I've been kidnapped. All I remember is that I was at the park by myself and suddenly everything went blank. I hear music from the front of the van and a man on the phone. I tried to scream but I can't be heard. I feel the van stop and the man gets out of it. I pretend to be passed out, he picks me up and goes into a large building. He puts me on a table and walks away. I lie in fear.

## Brooke Whetstone (12)
Caludon Castle School, Wyken

# Trapped In Killing

I didn't choose this life. It just happened. I was offered a lot of money to dispose of my two-year-old cousin. Then killing became something I liked. As I was on my way to my next kill, something caught my eye on the side of the road. I went over to take a better look and realised it was a knife. It was soaked with blood. I took a closer look and knew it was a knife I had used a few hours before. Not knowing what to do, I panicked and ran away with it.

**Javier Vassell (11)**
Caludon Castle School, Wyken

# Trapped

Trapped... I am trapped in a coffin. I can see utter darkness. It smells of old people. I try shouting for help but I keep breathing in dust. I think a funeral service is going on and it sounds sad. I want to burst out right at that moment to prove I'm alive still. All of my relatives are sad and crying, just imagine how they would feel when I burst out alive. They will burst out with tears of happiness when they see that I am alive and very healthy.

**George Green (12)**
Caludon Castle School, Wyken

# Trapped

Oh no, I'm trapped in an abandoned house and it is really scary and ark. I don't know what to do. The door is open but I am upstairs and there is something on the stairs that fell from the top. There is no food or drink anywhere and the only way out is to jump out the window but that is like 20 feet down and I'm not jumping that far down. There is no one in sight but I can hear loads of noises like talking downstairs...

**Kathan Hoban (11)**
Caludon Castle School, Wyken

# Trapped

That was it, the gate was locked. We had nothing. All we had was each other. We couldn't call anyone because our phones were dead. We tried to log on to the computer but they were locked so nobody could log on. Then there was a massive bang on the door. We all hid under the table. Then all the lights turned on. We all screamed, then the lights went off again and it was morning. I was in my bed, it was just a nightmare.

**Ava-May Davies (11)**
Caludon Castle School, Wyken

# I'm Trapped In A Video Game

Reliving the same level all the time, I'm stuck here in this nightmare, terrified. Playing this video game every day. I'm this same character all the time and I still don't know how I got here. Please send help. The concrete floor rumbling every time I lose a life. I'm trapped and I still need to wait 67 hours until I can try and leave this place.

**Sienna Nestorenko (11)**
Caludon Castle School, Wyken

# Death

The lift stopped suddenly. The lights went out, blood appeared on the ground. The people in the lift disappeared into the shadows. I felt like I was in a horror game. I tried to conceal my emotions, however I couldn't do it. Suddenly I saw an ebony figure emerging from the shadows. A dark ominous figure enveloped the space around me. I felt petrified...

## Hasan Tahir (11)
Caludon Castle School, Wyken

# Imprisoned

There isn't a person alive who doesn't fear being closed in, fear being imprisoned in eternal darkness. Imagine if you were trapped for as long as you remember; never seeing the light of day. Imagine if you were confined within the walls of your own mind, always searching for ways to escape but never succeeding. It seems as if the clock has been counting down forever. I don't know why but I'm about to find out. Three, two, one. I brace myself as the door swings open. "It's time to take your medicine," says the shadowy figure that enters.

## Alicia Banton (13)
Chellaston Academy, Chellaston

# Trapped

That's the title. Usually when you read something with the title 'Trapped', the character might be mental. Everything's in your head, that you have a problem. Never. Everything is real. 100%. I think... I think I was kidnapped. I found myself in the car boot. Yeah, I know this car. It's our car. I sit upright and bang my head on the fake hard cushion above me and lie back down again. I wait. I hear them. Talking? Yes talking. Wait, no! Arguing. I roll towards my only escape, which isn't very far, then kick it open and roll out...

**Anna Moseley (13)**
Chellaston Academy, Chellaston

# Time Till We Die

In this world time is trapping you, it's following you everywhere you go. It's all you think about. I look down at my watch, three hours. If you don't know me yet, I'm Lucy, have one brother and live in a world where time is how long till you die. Mine says three hours unless I can find a time booster which will give me another seven hours. Our world is divided into twelve sections, my section doesn't have a time booster. So I need to go to a different section but that might cause death, as sections don't agree...

**Lucy Cripps (12)**
Chellaston Academy, Chellaston

# Trapped

I awoke to my head throbbing violently, all I could see was nothing. I tried to take a step but I was held back by rusting chains. There was suddenly a distant repetitive tap of footsteps. I could tell they were gradually getting closer and closer until a door swung open. Light pouring in from it. In the glow from the door stood a man. I immediately looked away from him; I knew he was the person responsible. There was nothing I could do, nowhere I could go. I was trapped. "You're safe now, nobody can hurt you," he grinned.

## Theo McKeown (12)
Chellaston Academy, Chellaston

# Trapped On A Bus

I was on the bus on my way home from school. Quite a lot of people were on it. All I had was my bag with food and water. I found my phone in my coat pocket so I played on it for a while seeing as the bus had free wi-fi. Then suddenly the bus came to a stop and everyone disappeared. I looked up and the steering wheel started to move. It was pitch black outside. So I looked at my watch. It was midnight. So I called home. I had no signal. I was stuck forever.

**Maria Baum (11)**
Chellaston Academy, Chellaston

# The Slave Trade

*Bam!* I woke up, banging my head on the person above, before swiftly apologising. My eyes quickly tried to adjust, yet seeing nothing. It was as if a blanket of darkness had covered every corner, every crevice of this unknown vessel. Then, suddenly, I heard voices. A door creaked open, slightly, filling the room with light. What I saw next was truly horrifying. Hundreds of Africans, each with shackles around their arms and legs, many starved, some scorched, some with sores covering their bodies. One man, the white man, stood above us all. I remember. Always beware the white man.

**Zoe de Palma (12)**
Rosebery School, Epsom

# The Dogs Of War

I'd made a mistake. The dogs were closing in. Faster, faster! Brambles clawed at my face, my arms, my legs. I scrambled up a tree and they surrounded me. I would not give in. But I had to... My palms were sweating. "Come down. Give up," D-7 called, and the others cackled in delight. I knew what they'd do to me. I wasn't stupid.

"The hard way it is," chuckled D-1 sadistically. They aimed their plasma blasters at me, and seemed to freeze in time. War emerged from the undergrowth. He pointed a solemn finger at me. "Kill the girl."

## Sylvie Martin (12)
Rosebery School, Epsom

# The Valley Of Magic

The crack of bones beneath my feet, the smell of rotting flesh. I've now been stuck here for five months, maybe six. I can't remember. Every day a bucket of gruel and a glass of water appears, I don't know where from. They're just there when I wake up. I am so tired, I can't stay like this for much longer. I was hunting for the Valley of Magic, but I was caught when the spell was cast and I fell through the ground to this chamber. One thought keeps repeating in my mind. Can I save my family?

## Emma Glencross (13)
Rosebery School, Epsom

# Prison Guard

As I pace back and forth, swinging my baton, the inmates in neon orange overalls scream, shout and bang on their bars keeping them in their cells. I don't even know how I got a job in the most secure prison on Earth. All I have to do is make sure they don't escape. Easy enough, right? Well I thought so too. Until one day when I was a little more exhausted than normal, I didn't check the food properly. I didn't even realise something was off until I heard a rattling like a key in a lock...

**Lauren Light (12)**
Rosebery School, Epsom

# Darkness

"Argh! Help! Ouch! Wait, where am I? It's all... dark. I should go and look for a light. Hmm... there's no light. This is very odd. One moment I was walking back from school and the next, I am here! What is that? Is anyone there?"

"Well, well, well," said a mysterious voice.

"Who are you?"

"Don't you know? I'm surprised at you, Kelly," answered the mysterious voice.

"Mum?" asked Kelly doubtfully.

The voice laughed. "Well done Kelly!" said Kelly's mother, whilst turning on a torch.

"What was that for?"

"Don't you remember?" said Kelly's mother.

"Oh yeah! It's Halloween."

**Branwen Parker (11)**
Ysgol Garth Olwg, Church Village

# Trapped

"I couldn't move," said a little boy named Will, he was seven. "A scary kidnapper came and took me on Friday 13th July." It was the 17th July now. The kidnapper has been very suspicious lately. He'd been walking around my neighbourhood and bringing more kids back with him. His name was Keith. Keith was 36 years old. "I have a question for you Keith."

"What is it Will?"

"Why are there gates if there's nothing out there?" said Will.

"Well," said Keith, "there's a certain reason and you'll never find out."

"Please can you tell me Keith?"

## Tia Edwards (11)
Ysgol Garth Olwg, Church Village

# Trapped

Without warning, the boy's eyes grew heavy then fell fast asleep. His heart pounding, he felt himself slipping into the treacherous memories called his dreams. Cursing words stabbed him in the ears and tears of burning sadness slithered down his cheeks, reminding him of all the repulsive things he went through. Suddenly, his eyesight went blank. From out of the shadows appeared the figure he feared most, his father. "You're a disgrace to our family!" he yelled. "You can't escape what you were brought into!" The shadow disappeared, leaving him alone, and the darkness dropped into a deadly still silence.

**Thea-Grace Sims (12)**
Ysgol Garth Olwg, Church Village

# Trapped With A Clown

I'm trapped in a cave! "What do I do?" Rocks coming down, blocking the entrance. "Oh no I'm trapped." This is so terrifying. *Splash!* "What was that?" more rocks come down. "What am I meant to do?"

"Help! Help!" I hear.

"Hello?" I shout. I run over to see what is there. "Argh it's a clown! Go away!" I screamed. It comes closer and closer. I throw a rock at the clown.

"You can't go anywhere," says the clown in a horrifying way. "Go away, go away," I shout. The clown is winning. "Help, help!" I say.

**Megan Evans (11)**
Ysgol Garth Olwg, Church Village

# Trapped In Time

I'm stuck, I'm lost. All I remember is putting batteries in my clock, then *boom!* Now I'm alone. My dog Rolo whines. "Oh and I've got you." This dimension is like the book I've been reading, Harry Potter and the Goblet of Fire. There's magic everywhere and I'm concerned for Rolo, he's speaking English and he's very hungry. All he's saying is, "I'm hungry." The portal's closed and there are all manner of creatures. There's a door that looks familiar. I run with Rolo. There's a crowd. I push through. I need to get home now!

**Catrin Fowler (11)**
Ysgol Garth Olwg, Church Village

# Trapped

I can't contact anyone for help. All I can do is sit and wait for it all to be over. It's boring being alone. Just waiting for them to bring food. My friends will be worried about me. I haven't talked to them in ages. Oh my god, the time has flown, only a little bit left. The computer is dead so I can't use that. Maybe I can write down my concerns and let them out the window. There. *Sigh.*
"You're grounded, deal with it."
"All I did was text my friends in bed."
"That's against the rules!"
"Seriously?"

**Alice Hanks-Doyle (12)**
Ysgol Garth Olwg, Church Village

# The Cave

I couldn't move. I was trapped in a claustrophobic cave. I've been here for about ten days without food or water. "Help me!" I screamed.

Suddenly a voice came out of nowhere, saying, "Leave if you want." It felt like I was stuck in a dark, claustrophobic room. But I wasn't alone. Yet again there was a voice saying, "We are watching, we always will be."

I shouted with all my strength, "Who are you?" I had no reply. The cave was getting smaller and smaller every second. I shouted again but louder...

Then I woke up from a dream.

## Sasha Gardiner (12)
Ysgol Garth Olwg, Church Village

# An Odd Saturday Night

"Help, help!" Bella shouted as she fell through the big dark hole. It was a Saturday night in Fairy-Tale Garden. Bella was getting ready for bed as she fell through a random dark hole in her bedroom. Mum and Dad were down in the lounge and couldn't hear Bella. "Help, please! I'm trapped!" Bella shouted at the top of her lungs. Mum came sprinting up the stairs.
"Bella?"
"Mum, Mum, oh thank god you're here."
Mum lifted Bella up from the rusty old dark hole. "What are you doing there? You're supposed to be in bed!"

**Begw Williams (11)**
Ysgol Garth Olwg, Church Village

# Trapped

I couldn't move. I was stuck, I kept replaying the moment it happened in my head. Olivia's scream when the car flipped. Suddenly I heard a familiar voice, mother's voice. She was talking to someone, but it wasn't me. Another woman but I couldn't recognise the voice. "She was in a car with the other girl, sadly she has passed." Oh no, who was she talking about? It couldn't be Olivia, it just couldn't. Suddenly the voice spoke again. "This one's in a coma, we're not sure how long it will last." Were they talking about me? Am I alive?

## Cadi Evans (12)
Ysgol Garth Olwg, Church Village

# Trapped

1,830 days I've been here, still no way out! What did I do to deserve this? There are locked doors everywhere and I hear a girl screaming. I don't remember how I got here. I miss my family and my friends. Why can't I go home? I want to go home. "I think I hear someone coming," said a girl.
"Why were you screaming and shouting young girl?" said a creepy old man.
"I'm sorry, don't hurt me," said the girl.
"You're lucky, next time I'll kill you," said the creepy man. Then he left. The girl started to cry.

**Violet Hammerton (13)**
Ysgol Garth Olwg, Church Village

# Last Hope

I didn't know what was going on. The only thing I could see was darkness. I started to hear screaming, it sounded like my sister and I wondered to myself *how do I get to her?* I reckoned it'd been a few months since I'd seen something or someone. I felt alone and as if I was trapped with no hope. I couldn't move, the screaming came back but I couldn't help but listen to what they were yelling. "We're losing her!" and "No, I can't say goodbye, she's my sister." Suddenly the screaming stopped, along with my faint heartbeat.

## Amy Hammond (12)
Ysgol Garth Olwg, Church Village

# In A Coma

"Jane, happy 21st birthday. You haven't woken up in nine months now." I heard my mother's voice, but I couldn't see her. I could hear she was holding back her tears. I wanted to say, "I love you" or "Don't cry." Had it really been nine months? I'd given up counting the days by then, I couldn't count them anyway. My entire world was just black, all I could do was listen, I had no choice but to listen.
"I miss you, please wake up." My mother couldn't hold back her tears anymore. Please. I just want to wake up.

## Hanna Rees (12)
Ysgol Garth Olwg, Church Village

# The Worst Day Of My Life

It's happening too quickly... "Run!" someone cries as the massive building was collapsing. Why does this have to happen? Why did someone bomb our flats? I'm nailed, I can't get out. "Dad?" I yell, knowing he isn't there. It feels so real, please don't be real. I can't call him, my phone's on the other side of the room. I can't say bye to him. At the end of my soul. The ceiling's about to collapse. When will this ever stop? "Aargh!" It is now a blackout.
I wake up in the hospital after a day. This is now war!

**Gwennan Deavall (12)**
Ysgol Garth Olwg, Church Village

# Inside The Garden Shed

*Bang!* The shed door slams shut. Candles flicker on a rickety table. I hear a whispered voice, I spin around and spy a peculiar man sat in aqua blue robes, peering at me through his thick glasses. "What are you doing here Brynley?" he bellows. I step back in surprise. Something croaks. Out hops a bearded frog! I'm confused. "How did you get into my shed and what are you doing here?" I ask curiously. He rises from his seat and says, "Welcome Brynley, you've stepped into my magic shed and now you have to stay." Oh no! I'm trapped!

**Brynley Davies (11)**
Ysgol Garth Olwg, Church Village

# Trapped

What happened? One minute I'm on a train, the next I'm in some place with old-fashioned people! Walking around or getting a horse to pull them around, where are the cars and aeroplanes and trains? This is so weird, it's as if it's 1850 or something! Right, I'm going to go ask one of the people in weird clothes what on earth is going on. "Excuse me miss, why are you wearing silly clothes?"
"How rude! This is what people wear in this wonderful year of 1851!"
I can't believe I didn't realise that I'm trapped in 1851.

## Isla Powell (12)
Ysgol Garth Olwg, Church Village

# The Goats

"Baaa!" The blood-curdling bleet roaming the cities, sharing the virus, turning humans into zombies, animals into vicious creatures. I haven't been outside for days. I only have some food and water left. I'm trapped inside. This morning I woke up to banging on my door. It was the zombies and goats. They were breaking down the door.

I ran to the bunker, locked the door, trying to find a cure. I found it! I stopped the virus. So the people that got evacuated could return home. Everyone stayed inside for a while just in case. Hopefully that's the end!

## Brooke Ward (11)
Ysgol Garth Olwg, Church Villiage

# Trapped In An Elevator

Once there were four girls going shopping. Then they decided to go in the elevator. Then the elevator suddenly stopped! They were extremely terrified, one of them was claustrophobic. She could barely breathe. Everyone else tried calling people but there was no service. They wouldn't stop shouting. They continued to shout for the next two and a half hours. Then they stopped shouting because they were out of breath. They were just sitting there for another two hours. Suddenly the elevator started to work. After that they continued their sleepover and had a lovely time.

**Tamia Davis (11)**
Ysgol Garth Olwg, Church Village

# Trapped

In 1996 a boy went into an old abandoned building and there was a machine. The boy turned it on and this portal appeared. He got his friends Joe, Tom and Bill and they went through the portal. They were in 1943, stuck in an abandoned building, they realised they were stuck in the past. "Oh no, we're stuck in the past!"
Joe said, "The portal's broken."
So they left the building and Bill said, "Let's split up and search for parts for the portal." They found the parts for the portal then started it up and went through...

**Owen Jenkins (11)**
Ysgol Garth Olwg, Church Village

# Trapped In 2020

The year of 2020. Locked away from the world. No school. No work. Everything online. Things getting worse and worse by the day. Months go past and people are sick of it. Why won't this virus go away? Coronavirus, putting our lives on hold. Stopping us from going outside. Stopping us from seeing people face-to-face because we still can't go outside. But this didn't stop us! We kept on going. People turned to Facetime and Zoom. And we didn't stop. And even though things started to get back to normal, we were still trapped. But we're never stopping.

## Lauren Knight (12)
Ysgol Garth Olwg, Church Village

# 1,142 Days

1,142 days I've been waiting to escape this horrible coma. Dark, empty rooms always watching me. I can't move, my arms stiff, legs numb, my eyes getting weaker by every second of the day. Every day gets worse. I've been trapped inside this nightmare. Still bruises and pain from the car crash 1,142 days ago. Glass all over my body, but it feels as if the glass is inside me, cutting my organs, killing me, destroying this imaginary nightmare. I can still feel my seatbelt stuck around me, but it gets tighter and tighter. Nightmares stop eventually, right?

**Talis Vining (12)**
Ysgol Garth Olwg, Church Village

# Trapped In A Museum

There was a school trip today, all the children were excited but one, Caitlyn. She was very bored and not interested in the facts and pictures of the olden days. She went around the pictures and saw a weird picture. She walked towards it and everything started to move on the picture and it went black. Caitlyn opened her eyes and noticed she was trapped in the picture. "Help!" cried Caitlyn. A few minutes later she heard kids laughing. She opened her eyes and noticed she was dreaming all that time. She felt embarrassed but at least it wasn't real!

**Jessica Mills (12)**
Ysgol Garth Olwg, Church Village

# I'm A Person, Get Me Out Of This Haunted Trap

1,142 days into this haunted trap with the predator, who's like a zombie. He protects the entrance, this is a nightmare. He walks around constantly, it's annoying. I know though that if I make a wrong move that he will hurt me! He keeps me locked up in a jail cell in the basement. He only gives me cold beans and rice. It's like I'm in a loop, constantly repeating and repeating. I'm getting sick of having the same thing over and over again. It's like a massive loop. No! I've started to repeat myself. I'm trapped in this loop!

**Keilan Bryn Harris (12)**
Ysgol Garth Olwg, Church Village

# The Lost Dog Who Was Never Found

One cold night my dog went missing. I changed into some running clothes and me and my roommate ran out the door and started calling for her, but there was nothing. We phoned the police but they said they couldn't help. My roommate was knocking on every door. Suddenly someone answered the door. We chatted for a while. "Come on in," she said. Out of nowhere every door and window locked. The woman ran and we didn't see her for a while. "Help!" we screamed, but nothing. Finally the police came. The lady was sent to jail, but no dog.

**Caitlin Rees (11)**
Ysgol Garth Olwg, Church Village

# Trapped In My Thoughts

"Help!" I cried. A black cloud stood over my head with negative thoughts and insecurities. There I stood shivering in fear. I was stuck, stuck in my thoughts. It was a deadly cloud of my thoughts. The cloud shouted out every negative word I'd said about myself, every insecurity I had. "I hate it!" I screamed. Oh how I wished it was a nightmare. I screamed once again and suddenly the cloud became brighter and then the cloud started to shout the good memories and the good stuff, but then... someone woke me up. I was relieved with joy.

## Alys Williams (12)
Ysgol Garth Olwg, Church Village

# The Dark World

I couldn't move... Then suddenly I heard a voice inside my head. "We're watching you." I was trapped inside a dark world with only me and dark demons who wanted to murder me, but I had an ancient wrist band. Unfortunately it couldn't protect me from an ancient curse that slowly destroys your flesh. Only one way out. I had no idea how to get there. The random journey felt never-ending. There's no way I could escape but as I finally arrived I had almost completely faded away but I made it through to find an even darker world. No!

## Harry Barrett
Ysgol Garth Olwg, Church Village

# Zombie Apocalypse

It's been 1,387 days since I've been able to move. I've been trapped and I can't get out. I'm in a zombie apocalypse and I can't get out. Time is running out and the zombies just keep coming. It's like I'm in a game. I'm on the roof of a wrecked van. There is loads of fire. All of my expensive clothes are ripped because of the attack. I'm keeping the zombies away with a giant windscreen wiper I got from the van and I'm also using the van's wheels as a shield. This is an extremely scary zombie apocalypse.

**Tomas Norcup (12)**
Ysgol Garth Olwg, Church Village

# The Room

It's been thirty minutes but it feels like it's been hours. I'm trapped inside this big dark room with nothing but a creepy bear on a rocking chair just staring at me. The room shrinks every minute, I don't have much time. I need to find a way out. I've checked the ceiling and the floorboards, there's absolutely nothing. I'm not going to get out in time. Wait, the bear, there has to be something inside. I have a knife in my pocket, I can cut open the bear. I've found a button. I push the button. It's a simulation!

## Finlay Hawkins (11)
Ysgol Garth Olwg, Church Village

# In Hell

I'm in hell. At least I think I am. People are screaming, blood-curdling screams that burst your eardrums. But all I can do is listen. There's a piece of cloth covering my eyes, and my ankles and wrists are bound by ropes. The smell of sulphur has filled my nostrils to the point of me going noseblind. My stomach is empty as I haven't eaten since I arrived. No matter if it is or isn't hell, it's my hell. Today the screams stopped. Then I started screaming. The reason is the fact that I now hear laughing instead. Getting closer...

## Ellie Ryan (12)

Ysgol Garth Olwg, Church Village

# Eye Of The Tiger

The year 2020 was the worst year for humans. Lockdown, quarantine, isolation, but for me it was one of the best. A chance to rest and recover away from the stares and glares of camera flashes. How the tables have turned! Now the humans will get to experience the lockdown life that has been mine since I was captured and torn from my stripped fellow felines and forced behind glass for the happiness of humans. Are they happy now? Behind their windowpanes, trapped. But for them, it won't last. If their prison-like treatment will end, why not mine?

## Sophia Grace Goulding (12)
Ysgol Garth Olwg, Church Village

# Alone

It's been twenty-two days since I've been stuck here. The days are repeating themselves and the worst part is I'm here all alone. Hi, my name is Amelia. At the moment I'm terrified. I have no idea where I am. It's been July the 21st 2019 for almost a whole month now. It all started at home for a family gathering, I accidentally dropped a vase full of flowers on the floor. Mum started shouting. I got mad and screamed, "I wish you weren't here!" I slammed my door and went to bed. And I woke up here. A dream?

## Grace Hawkins (12)
Ysgol Garth Olwg, Church Village

# Let Me Live

"Leave if you want to," Paul my kidnapper said, sounding fed up. I'd been here for months, why had nobody come for me? But most importantly why was he letting me go? I thought he'd kill me. He crept forward with a knife, maybe he was going to kill me. He laughed psychotically but before I let him hurt me I swiftly ran away from him. But he didn't chase after me. He dropped the knife and fell to his knees. I carried on running through the abandoned warehouse. Wow. My body was bruised and in excruciating pain. Why me?

**Charlotte Royle (15)**
Ysgol Garth Olwg, Church Village

# Elevator Emergency

Hello, I was trapped inside an elevator at night. I am not sure who but someone trapped me. I was not happy at all, I had an atrocious heart attack and I was panicking extremely badly. It was so bad that I almost died. I kept pressing random buttons and I was shouting for help. Nobody appeared until I pressed the emergency button. I was so stupid, why didn't I think of that? When the kind old man came he said, "Good thing I came because the elevator would've broken." I couldn't believe my luck. What a kind old man.

## Tomos Pritchard (11)
Ysgol Garth Olwg, Church Village

# The Zombie Apocalypse

Help, I'm trapped in a hole and I can't get out. I was walking on a mountain and fell into this massive hole. It's raining and I'm getting soaked. I can hear a noise, it sounds like a zombie, like 100 of them. It's very dark and I can't see anything outside, the only thing I can see is the lovely moon and the stars. I just heard a stick break right outside the hole and it sounds like it's getting closer to me. Can you come quickly please? I'm scared. I feel like I'm getting surrounded. It's here!

**George Baldwin (12)**
Ysgol Garth Olwg, Church Village

# It Lurks

Trapped inside this cave, this nightmare. It's keeping me in, locked up with my own fears and stress. There's no escape. I need help... It lurks. I hear my voice echoing in the darkness of myself, my thoughts, my mind. Make it stop! I'm not certain if it's just me. I tell my mother everything that she needs to know. She comforts me, she is concerned about me. She gives me advice, I take it. Freedom is near. I'm at its core. It tries to drag me back in, I resist. Freedom! But it's waiting for me. It still lurks.

**Oliver Andrzej Jenkins (11)**
Ysgol Garth Olwg, Church Village

# Down In Hell

I hate it here in hell. Sure I'm a demon but it's very boring, especially since I'm a purple demon while every other demon is red or black. I can't wait for my 18th birthday so then my true power arrives and finally show all the other demons that I'm invincible. *Boom!* My power has grown so powerful I- Wait, what's going on? I'm... argh! Wait, that was a dream? But... but that felt so real. *Sigh.* Well that was odd but hang on, this isn't my house. Where am I? Help! Oh no, I'm stuck.

## Gruff McCallionn (11)
Ysgol Garth Olwg, Church Village

# Trapped In A Forest

I appeared somewhere in the middle of nowhere, where I was looked like a deep dark forest. I tried to walk around but I was trapped, scared for my life. This person in a black hoodie came walking to me, in a deep voice they said, "Move!"
I said, "I can't."
He stopped and said, "What?" I was looking around because I could move my mouth and eyes. Then I saw it, a mirror. How random for a mirror to be in the middle of nowhere, so I looked int he mirror and I was shocked. There was nothing.

## Sam May (11)
Ysgol Garth Olwg, Church Village

# You Don't Want To Know

Once upon a time I went to the woods with some friends and suddenly they all disappeared with no trace. Then in the distance I saw three bodies. I ran. They were my friends. I've had PTSD since. Anyway, I looked for my phone, it wasn't there. I was trapped in the forest with something with me. Then this thing came at me and I asked, "What are you?" It answered, "You don't want to know."

I thought I was done for, but then it died and fell. My friends' ghosts were behind it. We smiled.

## Daniel Wright (11)
Ysgol Garth Olwg, Church Village

# One Of Them?

I went downstairs to have breakfast but I noticed something weird. My mum wasn't acting normal and that's when her arm came off and she was a robot. I peeled at the walls to uncover a dark and dirty house and saw a door. I ran towards it and it slammed shut. Then I heard somebody say, "Leaving already?" But I looked around and saw nothing, but then heard somebody walking upstairs. So I ran and listened for footsteps. By this time I realised it was a haunted hotel and at that moment I found myself lying down...

**Anika Richards (11)**
Ysgol Garth Olwg, Church Village

# A Rather Unusual Game Of Hide-And-Seek

Once upon a time, something quite weird happened to me. It was an average day and me and my friends were playing hide-and-seek. I was hiding in this tiny cupboard as I was somehow flexible enough to fit inside of it. They had finished counting a while ago and still hadn't found me. I was starting to get worried. I went to get out because they couldn't find me but the cupboard door wouldn't open. I tried to scream but nothing came out. I was trapped in a nightmare and I couldn't get out of it... "Help!"

**Lola Pugh (11)**
Ysgol Garth Olwg, Church Village

# Trapped

I'm trapped in a zombie apocalypse, only thirty seconds left until all the people turn into zombies, except for me. I'm in my house alone with a baseball bat in one hand and a knife in the other. There are now twenty seconds left until the people turn zombie. I'm very scared and nervous, I think I'm going to die. I'm trying to cover my house with traps. 10, 9, 8, 7, 6, 5, 4, 3, 2, 1... I'm not going downstairs. I hear loud bangs on my door and growling and screeching. One of them's in my house. Help!

**Freddy Gabe-Williams (11)**
Ysgol Garth Olwg, Church Village

# Floating

I've lasted thirty days out here, drifting through space and I'm running low on rations. The supply of oxygen is also running out fast. Most of the ship's power is out but NASA is trying to locate the shuttle that I am in. I suddenly find a signal to a nearby land or planet, but something is wrong. The bright, glowing red alarm goes off. It gives me a countdown from ten. I don't know what it's for. On the device in front of me it says, "Collision in 10, 9, 8, 7, 6, 5, 4, 3, 2, 1... *Boom!*"

**Dylan Corsi (12)**
Ysgol Garth Olwg, Church Village

# A Police Little Helper

I'm trapping a kidnapper's arms. The police put me on him. He's fighting against me. I don't know if I can stay locked onto him anymore. The police are dragging the kidnapper into the back of the van by pulling me. I'm on my way to prison in the dark eerie van while the kidnapper is trying to unlock me. I'm made of metal and plastic and I'm like a lock to help out the cops. I'm happy today because I have helped the police to get another nasty person out of the public. What do you think I am?

**Ifan Harris (12)**
Ysgol Garth Olwg, Church Village

# 300 Days

It's been 249 days since I was kidnapped by one of the biggest murderers of the century. I'm living in my kidnapper's attic with a sleeping bag and a few mice. The name of my kidnapper is Lesley Davies. I forgot to mention that I only have 51 days left to live unless I find a way to escape, which is unfortunately impossible as everywhere is blocked off. Lesley has already shown me the sharp, bloody and dangerous knife that will end my life. Since living in the attic I have spoken to not one member of my family.

## Seren Kyte (12)
Ysgol Garth Olwg, Church Village

# Gone And Never Coming Back

I once went on a walk after a stressful day at school. I saw an abandoned house in the middle of a wood I've always been too scared to discover. I entered the house getting ready for possibly the most horrifying moment of my life. I was in the house in silence looking at the gruesome building. I started crawling through the house, wondering how long it would go on for. After five minutes I realised I was trapped! It was going on forever and I couldn't find my way out. I'm still looking after another five years.

**Evan McCarthy (12)**
Ysgol Garth Olwg, Church Village

# The Prison With The Scary Guard

One day whilst driving fast, a very scary thing happened. So, I stopped and noticed two gates opening and I decided to walk through and then a pair of doors. Suddenly, the doors slammed shut behind me. Out of nowhere a man started grabbing me. I tried to run away by running up this staircase, but he kept following me. He chased me into one of the prison cells and he locked me in! "Oh no! I'm trapped." I heard the man walk off, whistling to himself leaving me here on my own, screaming for help whilst trapped.

**Morgan Pugh (11)**
Ysgol Garth Olwg, Church Village

# The Kidnapping Of A Boy

I've been watching this boy for a week. He is a target for John. Now is my time to pounce. First I break the living room window, take out his mum and run upstairs. It's nearly nine o'clock at night so he should be asleep. There he is in his bed. He looks about nine years old. I grab him by his pyjama shirt, run back downstairs and throw him in my van. He's out cold. I drive the thirty-minute distance and take him out of the vehicle. I'm at old John's shed. He's thrown inside. Now he is trapped.

## Harri Tudor-Asveld (11)
Ysgol Garth Olwg, Church Village

# The Kidnapper In The Black Cloak

1,142 days, I'd been here waiting for someone to open me, turn my handle and walk in the room. It's nice and quiet in my haunted house until someone bursts through me and chucked a dead body on the old creaky floor. It was that man I had heard and now he is dead. He smells stale and rotten and there are flies circling all around his body. The body's very tall and thin, dressed in a black cloak with long trousers and the most polished black shoes and white gloves, which are stained red from all his own blood!

**Madison Ranson (12)**
Ysgol Garth Olwg, Church Village

# Never-Ending Nightmare

There I was trapped between two walls. I couldn't move, I was panicking. My face started to sweat, the more I moved the quicker the walls caved in. I screamed for help but no one came. Suddenly I heard a voice, a deep and scary voice. It said, "Leave if you want to." I looked for an exit but there wasn't one in sight. Then I saw a strange shadow coming towards me. I wanted to run but I remembered I was trapped. The man was coming closer. I didn't know what to do to escape this horrible nightmare...

**Chloe Edmunds (11)**
Ysgol Garth Olwg, Church Village

# I've Forgotten

Darkness. The only thing I saw was darkness. The only thing I felt was darkness. I was trapped somewhere, I didn't know where or why. I heard water dripping and echoing around me. I was scared. I tried to feel for a wall or something so I ran straight forward but I didn't feel anything. So I kept running and running for what felt like forever. There was no end. Then I hit something with such force I was knocked out. I woke up and I realised I was tangled up in some pipes. I remember now, I'm a plumber!

## Noah Daniell (11)
Ysgol Garth Olwg, Church Village

# Trapped In A Dream

I was sleeping soundly before a nightmare came into my head. A nightmare that I will never forget! I thought that I would have been fine and I would wake up nicely, but I didn't. A monster at a haunted house. Things popping in and out of the walls! Blood and bones and skulls. "Argh!" someone screamed. Was someone there? I looked around for a little while. I saw nothing. I walked around the corner and I saw a door. A big oak door with an old-fashioned lock. My only way out. But... where was the key? Oh no!

**Awen Rhys (11)**
Ysgol Garth Olwg, Church Village

# Trapped

The room was dark, nobody around to see and then I heard a loud bang. I started running with a flashlight, going nowhere. I realised I was trapped. I started panicking and screaming until I saw my mum. She said, "It's going to be okay, I'm here now." My face went in shock because I knew my mother was dead. Something growled and barked at me, then I saw a wolf. Running as fast as I could, I lost the wolf then I fell into cacti. Screaming in pain I watched the room go dark, then realised I was dreaming.

## Scarlett Chard (11)
Ysgol Garth Olwg, Church Village

# The Box

My name is Ffion, I live with my mum and my little sister Darcy. She's a weird child, embarrassing too. The other day I was in my room when I heard loud noises coming from her room. As I crept across and burst through her door, Darcy quickly pushed a box under her bed. I asked her what she was hiding. She pulled out a key from her pocket and opened the box. Peering out was a bug-eyed head. Suddenly it popped out. I screamed and my jaw dropped as a tiny alien danced around the room singing, "I'm free!"

**Ffion Jenkins (11)**
Ysgol Garth Olwg, Church Village

# Little Timmy Goes To Hell

Little Timmy walked to the shop. Little Timmy saw an evil man dressed in black, holding a gun at Timmy's friend Jimmy, and he shot! But missed and hit Little Timmy and then Timmy woke up in a dark, scary place with volcanoes everywhere. He thought it was hell! An evil person named Death came over and said, "You're in hell and Timmy cried for weeks while he was locked in a cage and all he could eat was the dragon's dump. He was trapped forever. He made a knife out of a rock and tried to finally escape.

### Rhys White (11)
Ysgol Garth Olwg, Church Village

# I Regret This

"Leave," they said. I regret this, I really do. One stormy night I was staying in a hotel alone on my phone as usual, scrolling through social media. I came across this video, it was a game to play with an elevator. Me being me wanted to try this game. I followed the instructions and stopped on the fifth floor. An old woman walked in. I didn't speak. I was getting scared. I went back to the first floor but it took me to the tenth and the doors opened and there it was. I was trapped in another dimension.

**Isabella Fry (11)**
Ysgol Garth Olwg, Church Village

# Us

We're always there, always. We feed off your dread. We are faster than you, stronger than you. We will find you. We will haunt you. We have risen from the shadows. We are the Mangamars. We glide surreptitiously. We run vindictively at you. We will crush you. We will find you. We will pounce on you. Our blue wings swoop through the air. We will batter our icy beam on you, it will solidify you. You will be fastened in ice and we will make your flesh crawl. We will find you. We will kill you. We oversee everything!

## Lewis Pitman (12)
Ysgol Garth Olwg, Church Village

# Trapped

It's been 137 days since I've been stuck in this dark, small room. Barely have any food or drink and I'm surrounded by loads of bugs. My first days in the room, the room was a normal size but every day it seems to become smaller and smaller. Because I have been so hungry I have started to eat some of the insects and trust me, they are disgusting. The past couple of weeks I've started to hear voices coming from outside the door and it sounds like two men and a woman. If you are reading this, help me!

**Freya Scofield (12)**
Ysgol Garth Olwg, Church Village

# Trapped

Trapped is a word that still gives me shivers. I was on my bike when suddenly I heard, "Stop!" Before I knew it I could see darkness. It was a weird sensation. I felt disconnected but I could hear sirens. I could feel people's breath on me. Then I lay there for what felt like hours, maybe days. Suddenly I could see. It was blurry but it was sight. I could start to feel pain everywhere. I could not move. I just wanted to scream. Ahh! I felt trapped. It stopped. I could move. I'd had an awful crash.

**Evie Rock (12)**
Ysgol Garth Olwg, Church Village

# Buried Alive

It has been six days since I was buried alive. I got into an accident while I was driving and while I was at the hospital the doctors pronounced me dead. I am running out of time because the air is getting thinner and becoming harder to breathe and the coffin is slowly but surely filling with mud. I was screaming for hours hoping somebody was nearby and heard me, but sadly that was not the case. It was very unlikely for me to survive but one evening my mother came along that Tuesday evening and she heard me scream.

## Harrison Keetch (12)
Ysgol Garth Olwg, Church Village

# Timmy Bullies Jimmy

Once upon a time there was a boy named Jimmy. Jimmy was eleven years old and he was bullied by Timmy. Timmy was fourteen and he was very nasty. He was the bully of the school but for some reason he always bullied Jimmy the most. He once trapped Jimmy in his van. Timmy said, "I'll give you sweets if you go in my van," but he didn't give him sweets, he just punched and kicked him.

Yesterday my friend Billy saw Timmy go into his van but he stopped the van and said to Timmy to never bully again.

## Ehran Richards (11)
Ysgol Garth Olwg, Church Village

# The Graveyard

Wandering through the graveyard it felt like something was watching me. The air turned black all around me. Ice-cold fingers gripped my arms as I screamed, "Help!" All of a sudden I heard a tune playing from this huge shiny music box. I walked slowly towards it and it was giving me shivers. I fell to the floor and some spine-chilling creepy hand covered in dark red blood grabbed my leg and dragged me to this huge deep black hole. He tied me up on a thin piece of old rope over the top of the black hole...

## Lilly Davies (11)
Ysgol Garth Olwg, Church Village

# A Dark Doom

I only have a few minutes left to live. The apocalypse has won this battle. All the food and water went three days ago and so did my friends. Unfortunately, nobody is here to witness my greatest achievement of being the last person alive. Even if I did have enough supplies I would still die. I would have to land but there would be too many zombies waiting. When I was little I always wondered what it would be to have a job and what the world would look like... Wait a second, there's someone docking. Am I saved?

**Max McDonagh (11)**
Ysgol Garth Olwg, Church Village

# I Need To Get Out

Fifty years I've been here, I'm trapped. I'm running out of food. I have to get out of here. I'm trapped in my little house in the middle of the woods, and there are zombies outside banging, moaning and groaning. I haven't slept for a very long time because I'm trying to find a way out. I have been thinking for a long time how to get out but I can't think. The zombies might bang the door down soon. Oh no! They are ripping the door handle off. I need to run. Umm, out the window! Go, go!

## Mali Cotter (12)

Ysgol Garth Olwg, Church Village

# The Apocalypse

I was frozen in fear, all I could hear was the screams of the zombies outside my door. I had to evacuate or I would die. As soon as I regained control of my body I heard the door break down. I ran upstairs to find zombies climbing through the windows. I had to get out. I grabbed my gun and I just ran as far as possible. Eventually I found a supermarket that had been long abandoned. *It'll work for now*, I thought. I took the supplies and now I'm writing this. Hopefully it'll end. May 14th 3592.

## Gethin Brooke (11)
Ysgol Garth Olwg, Church Village

# The Escape

I've been trapped here for at least a month. Just staring at blank walls with nothing to do. I don't know who's trapped me or what I have done. The moment I tried to escape, argh! He caught me. It's now 11pm and everything is dark and I can't sleep with all the thoughts inside my head. Suddenly there is a whisper by the window. There is a person there to rescue me. I'm so thankful! I climb out of the window with the person running for my dear life. What will happen next? I'm so scared!

## Sophia Smith (11)
Ysgol Garth Olwg, Church Village

# The Ghost Town Airport

Oh no! Tom's flight was delayed so he had to sleep in the airport. He found a bench and he managed to drift off. Tom woke up and checked the time. It was 11 o'clock, but there was no music and nobody around like there was earlier. "Hello!" Tom shouted. There was no reply so he went to check the door and it was locked. He was trapped. So he went back to the bench where he slept to grab his stuff to go exploring. *Thud!* There was a crash in the vents. Tom had a look. It wasn't human...

**Will Thomas (11)**
Ysgol Garth Olwg, Church Village

# Trapped

I am trapped in a zombie apocalypse. 50% of the world's population is full of zombies! My friend Ben and I are both professional gunmen. We both have lost our family members to this apocalypse. We met at a gun shooting centre. One time when Ben and I were on our daily watch around the town, all of a sudden a swarm of zombies attacked us. Sadly Ben did not make it. So that made me more determined to destroy all zombies. So I convinced everybody to fight back against this madness. Luckily we beat the zombies.

**Daniel Jones (12)**
Ysgol Garth Olwg, Church Village

# Kill The King

I am stuck in this toxic relationship. I'm a princess, the queen to be. My parents are forcing me to marry this evil man. Apparently he's here to help the kingdom, but I know what he's hiding. George is very attractive, I'll give him that but as soon as my parents leave he starts abusing me. He never lets me go out alone or choose what I want to wear. I live in hell! All he wants to do is cruelly kill my father. I've warned them over and over again. Tonight he plans to do it, kill the king!

**Megan Phillips (11)**
Ysgol Garth Olwg, Church Village

# Trapped

I was locked in an old abandoned school, searching for a snack after not eating for a while. But I didn't find anything. All I ate that day was some crumbs in the bottom of my backpack and some warm water. After that I felt sick. All night I was shivering. I had no blanket, no pillow, no nothing. I thought I was going to die. Suddenly someone tapped me on the shoulder and I screamed and it was only some builders knocking down the school and building a brand new one for all the kids. Suddenly... I fainted.

**Lexie Wright (11)**
Ysgol Garth Olwg, Church Village

# The Time I Got Stuck In A Distant Dimension

It has been 240 days since I was teleported to this dimension by the portal generator I discovered in my basement. When I switched it on I got sucked through the portal. Here it is boiling hot and freezing cold at the same time. The air has an aroma like poison and also there are these flying demon things that are trying to murder me. If you are wondering how I'm alive, I'm hiding underground and I have a low quantity of food and water. I need to find a way out of this wretched place before I perish.

**Thomas English (12)**
Ysgol Garth Olwg, Church Village

# The Moon

My heart was racing as I tried to reach the ship, but I was too late, I was left behind! *How do I get off?* I asked myself. I only had a limited amount of oxygen left. I couldn't hold back the tears. I was cold and scared. I didn't know what to do. Millions of thoughts rushed to my head at once, like *did they forget about me? Is this the last place I will ever see?* I panicked and became frantic as everything started to become blurry and I felt dizzy as blackness finally fell over me.

**Eleri Gardner (12)**
Ysgol Garth Olwg, Church Village

# Trapped In Space

My name is John. I have been trapped in space for 506 days. I miss my family and friends. The oxygen is thinner by the day. I have no navigation. I'm getting closer to the sun by the day. I have control of the spaceship, but I am running out of fuel. My expectation of seeing my family once again is low. I have three meals left, so I decide to ration my food out.

The next morning I see a shimmering blue and green planet. It's Earth. I am over the moon as I enter the Earth's atmosphere. Help!

**Dylan Griffiths (12)**
Ysgol Garth Olwg, Church Village

# Trapped In A Movie

It was my favourite part of the movie, then suddenly I got sucked into the movie. Even my accent changed, and my outfit! This movie was also a musical so out of nowhere everybody started singing and dancing and I tried not to but my body wouldn't let me, it was like I was part of the movie. I tried everything to get back but unfortunately nothing worked. As the day went on I started to enjoy where I was because I was meeting new people and learning new things. Later that night I woke up back in reality.

**Seren Smith (12)**
Ysgol Garth Olwg, Church Village

# Trapped In A Cult

"We are watching, we always are." The rules are so strict I can't escape them. If you leave you will feel as if you are being watched. We are scared what they'll do. We are trapped in the group of our own friends. If you leave he will get you. No one knows where he is from or who he is, but still you don't want him after you. I feel cold sometimes when I think about the cult, but it's much worse when you have to meet up and your life is in danger. Please help, it's the cult.

## Jac Lewis (12)
Ysgol Garth Olwg, Church Village

# Childnapper

Thirty days I'd been here and no soul had come to find me in this dark, gloomy room tied up to a chair. I hadn't seen my kidnapper in a week. I hope I'm not trapped here forever, he even locked the door. But then he came back with a knife in his hand and grin on his face and my friend Madison who was all cut to the face. I shouted, "Help!" but no reply, until he whispered, "You may leave," in a croaky voice. He cut me out. I sprinted out to hear Madison screaming in pain.

**Harrison Thomas (13)**
Ysgol Garth Olwg, Church Village

# Trapped In Another World

Ahh! I've been here twelve days now, it's like another world. The clouds are grey and the ground is rough like hay. I just can't stand it. What have we done to the Earth? Pollution has taken over and corrupted people's minds. Everyone has lost it and I think I'm one of them. If only I could fix my watch, but no. There are no resources for me to harvest, or are there? For me to be able to fix it I need some screws and a bit of magic. Yes, finally, I fixed it. Now it's time to try.

**Alex Rutherford (12)**
Ysgol Garth Olwg, Church Village

# Trapped In Tuesday

This is a story of when I was stuck on the same day for however long. It felt like an eternity. This is the thing that happens in nightmares. It was an average Tuesday morning. I woke up to my alarm and went downstairs. I checked my socials then went upstairs to change. I then left for the bus. After a hard day at school I went home and had my dinner. I then woke up and it said, 'Tuesday' on my phone. Everything was the same as yesterday. I repeated the day many times until I awoke on Wednesday.

## Gwenllian Hadley (11)
Ysgol Garth Olwg, Church Village

# Darkness In A Forest

I was running in the forest before I was hit with something at the back of my head. Before I blacked out I saw a figure black as night behind me, then I blacked out.
When I awoke I was in a dark room, no windows, but there was a jail cell-like door in front of me. I was too big to fit through the gaps in the door. Suddenly a man appeared and he said, "I hope you're comfy because you're staying here for a while." Then he left, talking to another person. I think I'm trapped...

## Lydia Higgins (12)
Ysgol Garth Olwg, Church Village

# The Mask

Victor woke up to see he was trapped with a nail mask around his neck. If he moved the countdown would begin. Now the trap was triggered. He saw me and a lock. He tried to get me to open but he was just flailing against me, then some speakers started up. It was the offender. "Victor you must find the key of the mask or else." Victor frantically ran around the room until he found writing on the walls. *I, V, X, II.* Suddenly a safe dropped and he entered 1, 5, 10, 2 and he got the key.

**Elliott Barrett (11)**
Ysgol Garth Olwg, Church Village

# The Deep Blue Sea

I'd been out here for 1,273 days and was low on food and water. The raft was getting damaged. I could see something in the distance but I had no engines. It was getting late so I went to bed. In the morning it was gone. Over time I gathered scraps of wood and rope to expand the raft and build more sails. There it was again. I thought to myself, *it has to be a mirage.* But I started heading towards it. *This is going to be a long day,* I thought, but it got closer and closer until...

## Ruben Lewis (12)
Ysgol Garth Olwg, Church Village

# Hell In The Woods

One day two girls were camping in the woods. It was getting dark so they decided to make a fire. One went to get some wood and heard a horrifying scream and ran back. Her friend was gone with no trace. She started to panic and there was no light or signal. It was dark so she couldn't find her way. As soon as she was losing hope she saw light and started screaming. They came over in a black hood and the mysterious person spoke saying, "I know where your friends is." The hood came down...

**Menna Owen (11)**
Ysgol Garth Olwg, Church Village

# The Mysterious Hole In The Tree

Once I went on a walk in the forest. There was a tree with an opening. I took a step in the tree, suddenly I heard a thud. I turned round, the hole was closed by a hard wooden door. I turned around, there were elves standing there before my eyes. I was captured by elves! Was I in Elf Land? They were small and they had a very squeaky voice, and I didn't understand what they were saying. Two of the elves took my hand and dragged me. They dragged me to somewhere. I was petrified. What was happening?

**Elliw Porter (11)**
Ysgol Garth Olwg, Church Village

# The Haunted Room

I'm still stuck in this haunted room. It has been 1,428 days and all I can do in here is make a mess then clean it up. I got kidnapped when I was twelve and now I am fifteen and 333 days old. One day I was on my way to my friend's house. I walked and this strange van pulled over and said, "Do you want a lift because it is raining?"
I said, "Okay." Then he strangled me and put me in this room. I haven't seen daylight since.
Then one day a kind hero saved me!

## Lillie Thomas (11)
Ysgol Garth Olwg, Church Village

# Clifford The Mutant Dog

I was on a walk through the city of New York when I got pushed by a hooligan into a manhole. I looked up and it was my teenage mutant ninja dog. He said, "Woof."
I said, "Clifford the big red dog? No!" He left and I remembered I'd bought my chicken and bacon pastie, but it was soggy. I cried and cried and cried some more. I didn't know what to do, I was trapped in the sewer with rats and a soggy bacon pasty. So I sat there and I fell asleep, but never woke up again!

**Dan Thomson (11)**
Ysgol Garth Olwg, Church Village

# The Repeating Spell

I couldn't move when I felt a spell being cast upon me. That turned me into a hideous monster. I then realised I was stuck in giant steel handcuffs. Luckily I could use my monstrous strength to break out of them, but only a second later one of the guards shot me with a dart gun, then I slowly fell asleep.

I then woke up and I was in the same giant steel handcuffs. I was in before, then I realised not only the curse turned me into a monster, I was reliving the same day over and over again.

## Ablah McBean (11)

Ysgol Garth Olwg, Church Village

# Trapped

This started in Australia 2008, a group of boys went scuba diving. There were so many twists and turns they got lost in a cave. There was not a lot of oxygen in the cave and that wasn't good. Then suddenly the tunnels started to collapse but luckily they found a cave and in the cave was a man with wings of a small dragon. It looks like this hybrid has been living in the cave. He knew the way out. They all jumped on the hybrid's back and flew out, back on the beach. They never did it again.

## Alfie O'Keefe (11)
Ysgol Garth Olwg, Church Village

# Trapped

"Leave if you want to," they said, but I couldn't. I was at a circus in the middle of nowhere. But I left anyway. I just sat around. Later I went back in and nobody was there. The animals were running around and the circus was completely empty. Suddenly I heard a crack. Everything went dark. I woke up and realised the tent had collapsed and I had the decision to find my way out or wait to be rescued. I was there for hours and then I slept until I heard a really, really loud growl...

**Alexa-Rae Jones (11)**
Ysgol Garth Olwg, Church Village

# Trapped

Help me, I'm trapped in a prison for something I have not done. I've tried escaping but the guards are everywhere. They are watching me when I sleep. I hate being in prison. They said they will kill me in one month if I'm bad so I can't be bad. The dinners are the worst, I only like chips but everything is bad. Being in prison is bad. The prison cell is so small if I stand in the middle of the cell I can touch the walls. It's so small. There's nothing to do. Life is hard.

**Harri Jones (12)**
Ysgol Garth Olwg, Church Village

# Spooked

All I see is empty seats in this haunted airport. I don't know how I got here, it is mysterious in my mind. Currently I have been here for eleven hours, and I just appeared here with no trace whatsoever. I am only twelve and I can't even read a map to see where I am, or to locate my family. This place is eerie and substantially big. I try to eat but I can't. Suddenly in a quiet voice I hear a voice... I jump as high as a giraffe. I hear a, "Hello." I got really frightened.

## Maisie Westall (12)

Ysgol Garth Olwg, Church Village

# Trapped In A Dream

I was trapped in a dream, it was horrible. I couldn't figure out where I was, what to do or even how it happened. There was barely anything around me and I was alone, it was the scariest time of my life! Suddenly I heard a loud bang and everything went blank and I couldn't see or hear a thing. I was even more terrified, then there was a gate but there was nothing on the other side. I waited for a bit to see if anything would appear. Then it appeared! What was there? Do I take the risk?

## Eva Mason (11)
Ysgol Garth Olwg, Church Village

# Iron Bars

Hi, I'm James Rogers, prisoner 1215, and I'm an inmate at Blackgate Prison. My cell is dirty, smelly and cold. All I can eat is bits of rice. The reason I'm in here is because I killed a man in cold blood, with a knife. Blood splattered all over the wall. I was in a gang, but they snitched on me and before I could do anything, I woke up in this horrible cell. I saw the guards walk past every day, then they came in, grabbed me and I think they were taking me to a guillotine. Oh no.

**Evan Smith (11)**
Ysgol Garth Olwg, Church Village

# Friday The Thirteenth

A long time ago, on a misty, stormy night, I was walking frightfully under a humungous black cloud, watching sparks of lighting flash brightly in the sky. It was the worst day of the year. I was out on my own like a ghost in a spooky graveyard. I dropped my tiny, smashed phone on the floor. Before I knew it, I was kidnapped and trapped in a rusty dirty van on the high street. As soon as I opened my eyes I realised I was chained dreadfully to the back of the van that drove me to horrible hell!

**Samson Dossett (11)**
Ysgol Garth Olwg, Church Village

# Can I Make It?

I am in a spaceship. Oxygen is running out. I don't have much time left. The rest of the crew is dead. "I am the last one," I say to myself. I hurry and look for the samples my boss had ordered me and the crew to collect. I hear a giant roar at the lower part of the ship. My bones begin to shiver as the roaring continues. I waste no time searching for the samples. I find them as soon as I see the roaring mutated rat. I run to the escape pod and escape the horrifying mutation.

**Joshua Capper (12)**
Ysgol Garth Olwg, Church Village

# The Creature

Once upon a time there was a girl named Millie and Millie was an explorer and there was one specific creature she was after. It was called a Specasorous and a Specasorous was a very rare animal. It looked like a dinosaur wearing glasses and so Millie went to Canada and that was the place to find the creature. She started the hunt for the animal and she found the animal was about. She set up the trap and she waited until she caught the animal and she was forever happy and the animal lived.

**Eva Thomas (11)**
Ysgol Garth Olwg, Church Village

# Trapped

There I was in the dark, eating my chicken curry and then I saw a clown, who chased me. I tripped over a rock and he kidnapped me and took me to a room. The door slowly opened and there was the ninja turtles with a spare sword. I picked it up and chopped the turtles' heads off. Suddenly I could smell gas and I passed out.

When I woke up I was in a different room, tied to a chair with rusty nails. There was this timer on the wall, it started to count down. 3, 2, 1, *bang!*

## Nathan Evans (11)
Ysgol Garth Olwg, Church Village

# Kidnapped

I once was kidnapped by guys wearing a black mask, a black hoodie and a pair of black trousers. They wanted to kill me. They took me away in their car. They took me to a dark house. They met another guy there, they were chatting. They were going to take me somewhere else, they said to another house to meet another guy. So they chucked me into the car. They drove off. They were holding a gun against my head. They threatened to shoot me because I was moving so much, then they did shoot me.

**Connor Gee-Wing (11)**
Ysgol Garth Olwg, Church Village

# The Dark Room

1,146 days I have been here in this dark room with little food or water. I have become weaker and weaker every day. I could not hear anything or anyone. The room was silent. I could not see anything either, it was just a dark room. If you were to walk in a straight line there would be no ending. I was alone. There was no one to be seen. The last time I was seen was when I got off the bus from school and started walking home, and then the kidnapper streaked in and I was gone. Terrified.

## Gwenllian Campion (12)
Ysgol Garth Olwg, Church Village

# The Prison Guard

I am the prison guard and I keep lots of people in prison and stop them from escaping. This prison traps them in for 100 years and if they get past the security doors and try to escape I'm always there to take them back to their cell and they also go without food for the rest of the day. This prison is 100 miles away from the city so I work seven days of the week, then I swap with my friend Bob. There are always 100 prisoners here, there can't be more or less prisoners here.

## Sam Price
Ysgol Garth Olwg, Church Village

# Trapped

Only thirty seconds left until they come. They are here. I feel them in the kitchen. I see them. I'm going to let them look around and then I'll start. They have looked around and they are unpacking. Okay, I throw a towel. I throw a bar of soap. They run to the bedroom and scream. They run to the door but the door is locked. They go to the window and get out but the gate is locked. They run back in and are hiding under the bed. They run to the door again and I let them out.

## Alice Bell (11)
Ysgol Garth Olwg, Church Village

# Trapped

Once upon a time I went to my room and fell asleep, and I was in a nightmare! My English teacher had trapped me in the back cupboard. I couldn't breathe very well! She wouldn't let me leave the room, even when everyone else had left. I had to do extra work and write a 1,542 word essay about how nice she is. But one of the children came back early and she trapped us both. Then the headmaster saw and the teacher was fired. I then walked out. I was crying but I was also free!

**Grace Huish (11)**
Ysgol Garth Olwg, Church Village

# Trapped In A Realm

The spell was cast and *boom!* I was trapped. The ugly witch was glaring straight at my eyes. I was in a magic realm. I had absolutely no idea how I got there. All I knew was that I was trapped. There was no way out. I got trapped by the most horrible witch. She had bright green skin and a big wart on the side of her face. She had trapped me in a cave full of bats. It was disgusting. It was my worst nightmare come true. I really wanted to get out. I was screaming so loud.

**Lani Jones (11)**
Ysgol Garth Olwg, Church Village

# Chicken Factory

Once I was in my bed dreaming of a nightmare that I was trapped in a chicken factory. So when I was in the chicken factory I started eating all the chickens until they were all gone because I was very hungry. So basically it wasn't a nightmare, it was the best dream I've ever had because my favourite food is chicken. I didn't eat all the chicken, I took some home for my family, but most of it was for me because I love chicken so much. Then I woke up and I was so sad.

**Gracie Nuthall (11)**
Ysgol Garth Olwg, Church Village

# The Mystery Kidnapper

It was a Sunday night on the 12th February 2013. I was playing football with my friends and a man was dressed in black. We were on a football pitch with the lamps on and he walked over to the electricity box, opened it and switched it off. Me and my friends tried to find our way out, but no hope. We thought we were all dead, but no, he took two of my friends in a white van. I sprinted after the van but lost it. Moments after, the white van turned around and got me unexpectedly!

## Siôn Bowen (11)
Ysgol Garth Olwg, Church Village

# Trapped

Only thirty seconds left until they arrive. Then all of a sudden I hear a knock on the door and then someone screams, "Hello is anyone here?" Then they open the door and they are exploring the house. They go upstairs and find a room. I don't want them here so I throw a chair at them and they get scared and try to run out the front door, but I lock it. They scream and try the back door but I lock that door too. So they are screaming. Do you think they will escape?

## Nia Akers (11)
Ysgol Garth Olwg, Church Village

# Trapped In A Coffin

It was a Friday evening, it was foggy and stinky. I couldn't see anything and suddenly the fog was gone. I was in a coffin and then the coffin door automatically opened. I got up and I saw an obstacle course and I got out of the coffin and I tried it out. Then lava was rising and then I realised there was a timer on the clock. I was crossing the lava rocks and one rock was very wobbly and I slipped and my leg got burnt. My hand slipped off one of the rocks. I died.

**Keelan Hatton (11)**
Ysgol Garth Olwg, Church Village

# The Scary Tiger

Hi, I'm Sophie. Some weird things have happened to me lately. I went to bed one night, closed my eyes and suddenly I started to spin. It felt as though I was in some sort of tornado. All of a sudden it was dark and quiet. I tried to get up but as I was jumping out of bed it was light again. I looked around and I was in some sort of rainforest. I saw a huge tiger! I screamed but nobody heard. The tiger was huge! He looked at me angrily. Will I ever get out of here?

## Sophie Poucher (11)
Ysgol Garth Olwg, Church Village

# The Kids On Their Bikes In The Haunted Forest

I was with my friends on my bike with a bunch of lumps in a forest. I went to go up a jump and the jump moved. I crashed my bike, went over the handlebars. Next thing my friends came over to help me. They all asked if I was okay. I said, "Yes, I'm okay."

Then Rohan said, "Do you hear that?" We all said yes. Next thing we knew, everything started closing in. We all go on our bikes and tried to escape. Only a couple got out of the forest...

**Callum Hooper (11)**
Ysgol Garth Olwg, Church Village

# Kidnapped

I was on my iPad in this game and it sucked me in, then this crazy old lady shoved me in the boot of her car. We were driving for a long time. I was terrified. Then she stopped. I heard screaming. The boot was slowly opening, it was my chance to run, so I did. I ran as fast as I could but I think I passed out...
I woke up in this strange house, it was dark and it scared me. It stank. she came downstairs and scared me. She said, "This is the beginning!"

**Louisa Royle (11)**
Ysgol Garth Olwg, Church Village

# The Falling Dream

I woke up... and I couldn't move. I realised that my mouth wouldn't open. That was the moment when I felt the room I was in just drop. I looked down, the rope wasn't there any more. That confused me so I tried to scream and I could. Then it hit me. I was trapped in a dream. I was still falling so I tried to figure out why... I looked down just in time to see the ground as I hit it. I suddenly woke up, sat up straight and banged my head. Then, I smiled.

**Jack Pidd (11)**
Ysgol Garth Olwg, Church Village

# Trapped

I was walking home when I realised I was being followed. I called the police and they told me to stay on the phone. I was almost home when they put me in the boot of their car. I screamed and cried. The police told me to try to kick the back light. I did so and waved my hand outside the car until I noticed there was a paint can. I poured it out. I screamed out the car and a woman heard me and called the police, but the man crashed into her car and bashed my head.

**Leila Jones (12)**
Ysgol Garth Olwg, Church Village

# Haunted House

The spell was cast. All doors shut and were stuck. I was trapped in a haunted house. What do I do? I tried to get out the window but it was stuck. I realised there was someone staring at me. It was a man with a long beard. He was coming closer and closer. He swung open the door and ran upstairs but I was downstairs in the living room trying to hide behind the cupboard. He ran down the stairs and was looking for me. He found me. Wait. That was my grandad! Ha!

**Olivia Bell (11)**
Ysgol Garth Olwg, Church Village

# The Chase

It was Friday 13th 2006 and I was sitting in the forest waiting for my next prey. Then that's when I saw him, blonde hair, blue eyes. He was perfect. So I jumped from tree to tree. That's when the branch snapped. I fell, so I tried to get a good grip. I caught the tree but I thought he saw me, so I ran for him. He tripped on a log and fell. That was my chance so I pounced. I bit his arm away. But I was distracted and he got away from me to safety.

**Brooklin Baldwin (11)**
Ysgol Garth Olwg, Church Village

# The Never-Ending Nightmare

1,142 days I'd been here. There was no escape from this terrifying loop of events. It started with me watching a rocket go to the ISS. That night I went to sleep to not know I'd entered the world of nightmares. It was me, watching the rocket launch again. But it went bad. This time the rocket came down over Ponty, but before it hit, it opened a portal to another dimension. Then it split into fifths. It came down and put all of Ponty in flames.

**Gareth Church (12)**
Ysgol Garth Olwg, Church Village

# Trapped In A Car

I went to the shop and I bought a pizza and some sweets and a pineapple. I got home and I cooked my pizza and then I heard a noise, it sounded like footsteps! I went upstairs, he ran downstairs into his car. I followed him and he trapped me in his car. There was no way I could get out, it looked like he was taking me to an abandoned place. I was so scared, I didn't know what to do. I tried to pull out my phone to ring my mother, but he caught me!

**Finnley Walker (11)**
Ysgol Garth Olwg, Church Village

# The Hole In The Bathroom

I woke up somewhere, it was like a castle. I got up and went to the toilet as I had been out for so long. So there I was in the bathroom and I saw a random button on the wall. So I pushed it and the whole room turned upside down. So then I screamed for help and no one came. Then I heard a noise and I looked. There it was, the demogorgon, holding Harry's dead head, his whole face was open with red teeth. I ran off scared and didn't look back.

**Hannah Weston (11)**
Ysgol Garth Olwg, Church Village

# Trap

I went to explore a house the other day, but little did I know it was haunted. So then I got trapped inside the house and all ghosts and zombies came out of nowhere and were chasing me. Luckily we had a one-way flight to Miami because we wanted to move out there. But one day they found out where we moved to so now they are coming to find me. if you are reading this letter it will probably be the last one because they have found me. I'm scared...

## Dylan Szalkowski (11)
Ysgol Garth Olwg, Church Village

# Trapped

Only one floor to go. I was on my way to America. I was waiting in the lift and it was going up. I was going on holiday to America for the week and I was meeting my mother by the aeroplane. The lift stopped suddenly and I got so panicked. Was the door going to open in time? I was going to phone my mother but there was no signal in this place and I was going to be late again. I tried to open the door but there was no chance! Oh no! What could I do?

**Mari Roberts (11)**
Ysgol Garth Olwg, Church Village

# Trapped A Bee

I was watching TV and I saw a massive bee, so I grabbed a glass and tried to catch it but it was too fast for me. I decided to leave it for a while and it might come back. So I sat back down and it came back. I quickly got a glass and eventually got the bee. I didn't know what to do with it, so I carried it outside and let it back outside. When I walked back inside it came back, so I caught it again and put it outside and slammed the door.

**Anwen Winter (11)**
Ysgol Garth Olwg, Church Village

# Trapped

I drove up to this abandoned hotel. Little did I know it was haunted. I walked in but I didn't realise... the door had locked itself. I went in, the wallpaper was curling off the walls, it gave me the shivers. I went into the spooky lift but then suddenly the lift started to go down. There was nobody there, but there was a voice and it said, "Leave! You have thirty seconds or die."

**Lily Reid (12)**
Ysgol Garth Olwg, Church Village

YoungWriters®
Est. 1991

# YOUNG WRITERS
# INFORMATION

We hope you have enjoyed reading this book – and that you will continue to in the coming years.

If you're a young writer who enjoys reading and creative writing, or the parent of an enthusiastic poet or story writer, do visit our website **www.youngwriters.co.uk**. Here you will find free competitions, workshops and games, as well as recommended reads, a poetry glossary and our blog. There's lots to keep budding writers motivated to write!

If you would like to order further copies of this book, or any of our other titles, then please give us a call or order via your online account.

Young Writers
Remus House
Coltsfoot Drive
Peterborough
PE2 9BF
(01733) 890066
**info@youngwriters.co.uk**

Join in the conversation!
Tips, news, giveaways and much more!

**f** YoungWritersUK     🐦 @YoungWritersCW